The Adventures of Peanut t

Peanut marched in line
following his family.

March.

March.

March.

He was content as he marched.
Following along as best he could.

"Left foot. Right foot. Left foot. Right foot."

He'd sing to himself
as he marched;
following his
family, as best
he could.

He and his family came to a huge pond filled with beautiful blue, sparkling water. Everyone gathered around, taking their share of the refreshing water.

After having a good gulp of cold water, Peanut sat by the **bank**. He enjoyed watching his friends splash and play, but there was something more on his mind today.

"Come join us, Peanut!" His friend, Monty, shouted as he blew water into the air with his trunk.

But Peanut didn't move. He sat on the bank, alone and unsure.

Peanut looked over his shoulder to the jungle behind him. Oh how he longed to run through the great unknown. Oh, how he longed to roam farther than he'd been before.

"Peanut!" His mother sang his name, calling for his attention as his family lined up. Each with tails held by trunks, and the march began again.

"Left foot. Right foot. Left foot. Right foot." Peanut began to sing; following his family as best he could.
The next day went much the same way. Peanut marched in line with his family; tails held by trunks.

"Left foot. Right foot. Left foot. Right foot." Peanut sang, marching along.

He and his family stopped again at the blue, sparkling pond. Again, after getting his share of the refreshing water, Peanut sat on the water's bank and watched his friends splash and play.

Peanut turned to look over his shoulder where the jungle **beckoned** him to come. He turned back to his friends and family who were enjoying the water. Peanut looked back to the jungle once more.

"Maybe they won't notice if I'm not gone too long." Peanut thought as he quietly got to his feet, a little hesitant as he took his first step into the jungle; into the unknown.

Trees hung over Peanut's head as he walked through the thick greenery that was everywhere. Colorful flowers were blooming everywhere. Peanut was in wonder as he walked farther and farther away from the blue pond, where his friends and family played.

OOK, HOO, HOO, HAAAAA, HAAAAA!

He heard them before he saw them. He heard them and grew frightened.

OOK, HOO, HOO, HAAAAA, HAAAAA!

Two monkeys came swinging by, grinning wildly and hanging from vines.

"Hey cool kid." One of the monkeys said. "We haven't seen you before. What's your name?"

"Peanut," Peanut said, and backed away a little **hesitant** with his trunk tucked in towards his front legs.

"Hey, hey, it's cool." The other monkey hung upside down from his vines, opening a banana and taking a bite. With a mouth full he said, "My name is Ollie, and that's Hank."

"How can you hang upside down like that? Doesn't it scare you?" Peanut asked, turning his head to the side in wonder.

"Scare us? Why not at all, sometimes you have to turn upside down so you don't fall." Ollie began to swing back and forth. "You should give it a try!" He exclaimed excitedly.

"You turn upside down so you don't fall?" Peanut was **baffled** by what Ollie meant.

"Hanging upside down, you see the world differently." Hank let his arms fly free as he hung by his knees, swinging upside down.

"Give it a try." The other monkey pushed a sturdy vine in Peanut's direction.

7

"How?" Peanut asked, as he **hesitantly** caught the vine with his trunk.

Ollie jumped from his vine. He took the last bite of his banana and tossed the peel aside. "Throw your hands on the ground and kick your feet in the air." He exclaimed as he flipped into a handstand showing Peanut how easily it can be done.

Peanut followed, but kicked his feet so hard that he fell flat on his back. He gasped as he lost his breath.

"Did you feel it in here?" Hank, who was still hanging from a vine said as he shook his head, pointing to his heart. He flipped off his vine and straightened out his spine. "We'll teach you just how to do it."

It took a few tries, but in no time, Peanut was hanging upside down and felt the blood rushing to his head. His trunk fell over his face and hung to the ground. The ground was above him, the sky was below him. For the first time Peanut saw everything differently. "Wow." Was all he could say.

Both Hank and Ollie were hanging on a branch across from Peanut, dangling their arms. "Yeah," Hank said in agreement, enjoying the moment.
"Its like looking with new eyes."

9

Ollie began swinging back and forth from vine to vine excited that Peanut had joined in on the fun.

Peanut hung upside down until he could no longer see the sun over the tops of the trees. It was time to go. "So long new friends, I have to go."

"So long!" Both the monkeys chimed in at once, "Hang with us again soon." The monkeys joked and laughed as they began to swing from limb to limb off into the distance.

Peanut jumped from his vine and felt the world turn right side up. He began to walk, taking his new and fun discovery with him. Then he came across a turtle.

The turtle was sitting upright. His legs were crossed in front of him and hands were placed together. His eyes were closed and he was smiling.

Peanut was **intrigued**.

"Why do you sit in such a way?" Peanut asked,
lowering his head towards the small turtle.

The turtle slowly blinked his eyes open
and smiled at Peanut.
"This is the way I meditate."
He simply replied.

"Meditate?" Asked Peanut. "What's that? How do you do it?"

Again, the turtle smiled. "Come," he patted the ground beside him. "I will teach you."

"My name is Peanut. What's yours?" Peanut sat down on the ground beside the turtle, excited to learn something new.

"Walt," The turtle replied. "First, you cross your legs, like mine." Walt spoke with a wise, old tone in his voice. "Then, you place your hands on your knees or bring your palms together at your heart. Close your eyes and take a deep belly breath in." He **demonstrated**.

"That's it?" Peanut asked **skeptical**.

"To start." The turtle smiled as he closed his eyes again. "Now we sit in silence and allow the world around you to fade into the background."

Peanut closed his eyes, following Walt's directions and sitting in silence. A few seconds went by, Peanut peeked from under his eye lids at the turtle who still hadn't moved. "Now what?" Peanut asked.

Walt smiled in response as he opened his eyes. "Now we find stillness in our mind and our body. We find awareness and oneness with the universe. Let your thoughts fade."

Peanut sat in silence a little longer. His mind filled with thought after thought, after idea and idea. "I can't make my mind shut off to sit in silence." Peanut eventually said, breaking the silence.

"The idea is not to turn off your mind. Its to sit with your mind. Allow each thought to come. Thank it for coming. Then send it away." Walt explained without opening his eyes. "Try to follow each breath by saying inhale and exhale."

"Inhale." Peanut took a deep breath in. "Exhale" He gasped as he let the breath out. "Inhale." He sucked in a huge breath of air. "Exhale." He gasped again. "Inhale." Peanut began to repeat the cycle.

"Peanut," Walt interrupted. "Its easier to say it to yourself, in your mind, than out loud."

"Ohhhh," Peanut began his cycle over. Only this time he spoke silently in his mind. "Inhale — Exhale."

Walt's suggestion worked and before Peanut realized, he had sat in total silence and stillness with himself. He took one last belly breath in and fluttered his eyes open.

Peanut slowly made his way up from his seat. He kindly thanked Walt for sharing his meditation and he began on his way once again.

As Peanut began to walk he realized that he was at peace. His mind was calm, his body was relaxed. He breathed in the fresh air as if it were the first time he'd ever smelled it.

Peanut's ears were alive
with new sounds as he
explored even farther
away from his family
and friends.

TWEET! TWEET!

TWEET! TWEET!

Peanut noticed a small flock
of birds jumping and
tweeting.
He got closer to
get a better look.

"That's it little one!" One of the birds said to a small baby bird. "Oh, hello, there," She tweeted at Peanut. "How do you do?"

"Hello." Peanut smiled. "I'm Peanut."

"Nice to meet you, Peanut. I'm Margarete." She nodded at him. "Come on, now." Margarete turned back to one of the baby birds who was **perched** on a tree limb. "You can do it."

After a moment of hesitation the baby bird leaped from the tree limb and flapped his wings **clumsily**, yet safely to the ground.

"Well done, little one" She nuzzled her beak to the baby bird's beak. "Now, off you go. Give it another go." She shooed the little bird away with a colorful feathered wing.

"Aren't you afraid they won't be able to fly?" Peanut asked.

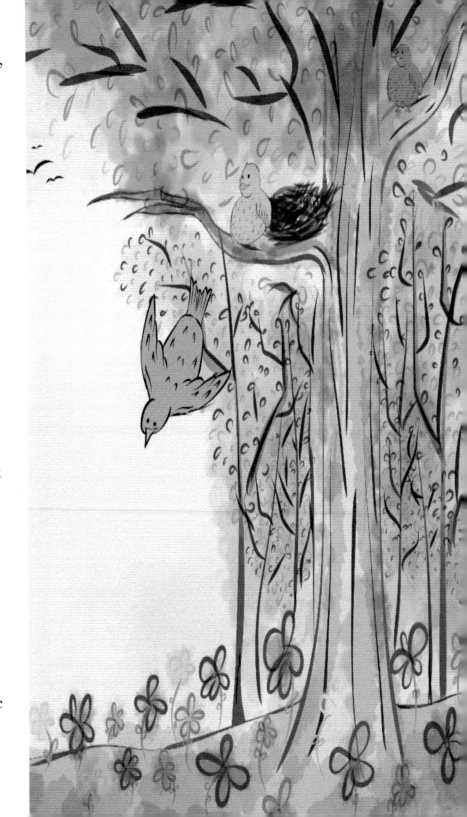

"No, not at all," She exclaimed. "You see, you can do anything. You just have to believe."

I can do anything. Peanut thought to himself. *I can do anything.* He repeated the thought again.

"Come on. You've got it this time." Margarete sang as she watched her little bird once again perched on a limb.

The colorful little bird spread out its wings, closed its eyes and held its beak high in the air. After a deep breath, the little bird leaped from the limb.

The little bird nose dived straight towards the mother bird. It's little eyes were still closed. Then, just at the last minute, it's little wings caught air and the little bird swooped back up towards the limb it had just jumped from.

"That's it little one!" Margarete jumped up and down, flapping her wings excitedly. The little bird landed safely back on the limb, chirping and jumping at the **accomplishment** of the flight.

"Way to go!" Peanut cheered. A choir of small birds, who were also learning to fly, began to sing as well. Chirping with **encouragement** at what their friend had done.

"Thank you." Peanut smiled at Margarete. "Now I must go." He turned and for the first time, he began to **confidently** walk through the jungle.

"Goodbye, Peanut," Margarete called and waved her wing. "It was lovely to meet you!"

Peanut waved with his trunk and a smile upon his face.

Peanut wandered his way through the jungle and came to a clearing where colorful flowers had followed him. Tall green grass held even more colorful flowers in a field in front of him.

Peanut was **captivated** by the scene.
Without thinking Peanut walked to the center of the
small grassy field and flopped down.
He rolled with his legs up and trunk out.
The sun was shining brightly
over the small clearing.

Peanut rolled over to find two bees sitting
on a flower buzzing loudly.
Both of the bees had their eyes closed.
As Peanut got a closer look he could see that
the bees were using their lips to make a
buzzing sound.

BUZzzzzzzzzzzz!

BUZzzzzzzzzzzz!

BUZzzzzzzzzzzzz!

One bee peaked one eye at Peanut.
"Hello, little elephant." He **acknowledged**
Peanut's presence, then closed his eye again.
"Oh, hello," Peanut responded. "What are you doing?"
Peanut inched in closer.
"We are breathing." The other bee responded. And they
both began pressing their lips together and breathing
through them again, creating a buzzing sound.
Their lips flapped together as the air rushed through.
"I've never seen breathing like that."
Peanut said.
"It is called Bee Breath."
The first bee explained.
"You can practice it,
even if you're not a bee."
The bee began
to laugh.

The other bee joined in the laughter. "Oh, he can do it. He's not a bee, but he can breathe like one."

"Do you want to learn the Bee Breath?" The first bee asked. Peanut nodded.

"I'm Carl." The bee **introduced** himself. "This is Beatrice."

"I'm Peanut." He paused. "What's the point of doing the bee breath?"

"Oh! So many reasons, where to begin?" Beatrice exclaimed.

"Let's teach you to Bee Breath. It's so simple, even babies can do it." Carl and Beatrice giggled again.

Both of the bees **perched** on the petals of the flower. "First, cover your ears," The bees stuck their front two legs into their ears. "Next, close your eyes." The bees closed their eyes. Peanut copied their every move. "Then, press your lips lightly together and breathe in deep through your nose, on the exhale, let the air rush through your lips. Your lips will flap together to create the buzz sound." The bees began to breathe.

Peanut was excited to follow along, and excited to learn something more. His lips flip-flapped together as he exhaled a breath.

"You just keep repeating this for several breaths." Beatrice peaked over to Peanut who was proud of his bee breathing.

The three of them sat there in the flowery field, flip-flapping their lips together, with their hands over their ears and their eyes shut.

It was sometime later that Peanut took his last Bee Breath. He sat still with his eyes closed for a few moments longer. His body felt light and tingly as the peaceful feeling Peanut had recently discovered only **amplified**.

After a few moments Peanut spoke, "Thank you for showing me how to breathe like a bee. I must go now." He got up from the green grass he'd been laying on.

"Goodbye, Peanut! It was wonderful to meet you." Carl spoke first.

"Yes, come join us again soon, Peanut,"

As he continued on his way Peanut came across a tiger. She stood with **poise** and confidence as she moved in a way that looked like a dance. The tiger moved from one pose into another, and then paused.

"Would you like to join me?" She asked.

"What are you doing?"

"Sun Salutations." The tiger closed her eyes and smiled at the sun. "I'm Joan."

"Hello Joan. I'm Peanut. What's a sun salutation?" He asked a little confused.

"Yoga poses that are **sequenced** together." The tiger began another round of Sun Salutations.

"What's yoga?" Peanut asked.

The tiger thought for a moment, still flowing through each yoga pose. "Yoga is a meditation in motion." She put simply, "Where each movement is linked with a breath."

Peanut was excited, as he had just recently learned how to meditate. "How do we do it?"

"Stand next me." Joan said. "Feet together, shoulders back, spine straight," She began walking Peanut through each pose.

"Inhale, reach your arms to the sky!" They both reached up high. "Exhale and fold yourself over." Peanut followed Joan's movement as they bent over to touch their toes.

"Inhale, lift up half way. Exhale fold over again. Inhale, step back to downward facing dog." Joan placed both hands on the earth and stepped both feet back. Her tail was high in the air. Peanut followed. "Inhale, reach your right leg up to the sky. Exhale, place it between your hands and reach both arms up. This is Warrior One pose."

They stood like this for several breaths before stepping back into a downward facing dog. Then, they began the yoga sequence again using their left leg. "It's balance. What you do on one side, you must do on the other side." Joan said as they flowed through the Sun Salutations.

After moving through the Sun Salutation several times, Joan stood with her feet together and her eyes closed. Peanut did as Joan and closed his eyes, but kept peaking at her from under his lashes. Finally Joan took a deep breath in, and let out a loud sign. "Thank you, Peanut, for flowing through Yoga with me today."

"Thank you, Joan, for teaching me Yoga."

Joan smiled a warm smile at Peanut. "Let's do it again soon. Now I must go. It was wonderful to meet you Peanut." Joan stretched her arms one last time by reaching out towards the sky before she pounced onto all fours and took off running.

Peanut closed his eyes and smelled the fresh air. "What a wonderful day this has been!" He said out loud. He started off again, along his journey.

Your turn to learn a # SUN SALUTATION

1

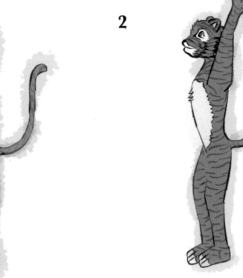

Mountain Pose

2

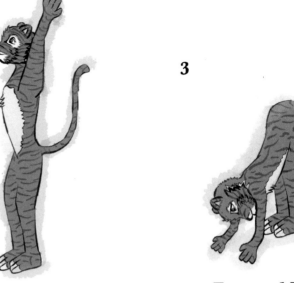

**Mountain Pose
Arms reach
towards the sky**

3

Forward Fold

4

Half-way Lift

5

Plank Pose

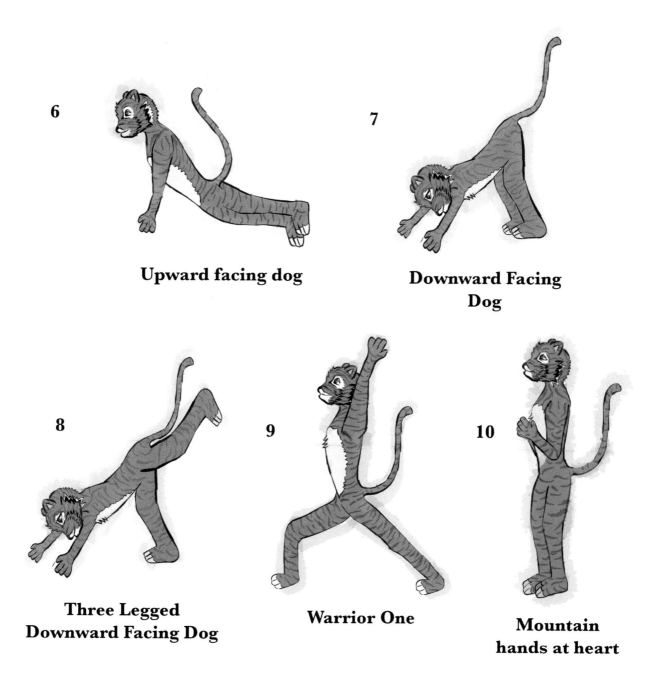

6 Upward facing dog

7 Downward Facing Dog

8 Three Legged Downward Facing Dog

9 Warrior One

10 Mountain hands at heart

Peanut noticed he was beginning to get thirsty
and he could hear water flowing a little ways ahead.

As he came upon the fresh water, Peanut could
see a frog sitting on the edge of the river.
The frog wasn't moving and his
eyes were incredibly wide.

Without a moments notice, the frog flicked his tongue out and grabbed a fly that was flying by. Then the frog was still again.

Peanut was fascinated. He waited and watched again. After only a short time of waiting, the frog flicked his tongue out again, catching another fly.

"You're quick." Peanut complimented the frog.

"Oh hello," The frog turned to Peanut. "I saw you sitting over there. How do you do? I'm Alfred. I don't believe I've seen you before." The frog eyed Peanut up and down.

"I'm Peanut."

"I'm afraid you've caught me at lunch time." Alfred turned back to face the water.

"Excuse me for interrupting you." Peanut turned to leave.

"Not at all, young fellow," The frog spoke, but didn't move and barely moved his lips when he spoke. "One," The frog whispered. "moment." He whispered again.

In the blink of an eye Alfred extended his tongue and caught a huge bug that was flying by. "Mmmm," He said as he enjoyed his lunch. Alfred dabbed his mouth with his fingers and licked them. "I've been patiently waiting for that one to fly by."

"I don't know that I could have waited." Peanut inched down towards the frog.

"All good things come to those who learn patience." Alfred explained. "Learn the art of patience and you will accomplish anything you desire." He jumped to a lily pad near by. "If you will excuse me, I go for a swim after lunch."

"Nice to have met you." Peanut smiled.

"I'm sure we'll meet again." Alfred nodded as he splashed into the water and disappeared.

Peanut thought for a moment as he took another sip of the refreshing water. Just as he was drinking he noticed two fish swimming along. Both of the fish were purple and their gills shined in the water.

"Hello, little elephant." One of the fish splashed water as his tail flipped through the pond.

"Hello." Peanut watched curiously.

"I'm Gil." One of purple fishes flipped over onto its back and waved with its tail. "Beautiful day for a swim isn't it?" Neither fish were watching where they were going, they just simply allowed the water to take them.

The other fish moved with the water and circled Gil. "I'm Finn. Won't you join us for a swim, little elephant?"

"Where are you swimming to?" Peanut asked.

The fish were still gliding, lazily through the water. "We don't know. We just go with the flow and allow the water to tell us where to go."

Peanut looked at the fish baffled. "Doesn't that worry you?"

"Not at all," Gil splashed. "Sometimes you just have to live in the moment and trust the process."

Finn chimed in, "Trust the process and go with the flow. You can't worry about what's up the stream. It won't do you any good."

Peanut thought for another moment before he stepped into the water and flipped over onto his back.

"That's it," Gil giggled.

The two fish and the elephant glided through the water, allowing the stream to carry them away.

Peanut was amazed at all the things he had discovered and learned. The sky was full of white fluffy clouds as he enjoyed the water and floated on his back. "I could take all of this back home with me." He thought out loud.

I can do anything. A small voice in his mind spoke. Peanut giggled in response.

26

"Peanut!" He heard a familiar voice.
He flipped over at the sound of his mother's
voice, surprised that the water had led him back
home. He waved goodbye to his new fish friends as
they continued along their way.

"Oh! There you are!" Peanut's mother rushed
over to him and wrapped him up with her trunk.
"You had me so worried. We've been looking all over!"

Peanut's friends and family gathered around.
"We're so glad you're back Peanut!" One of them said.

Loud trumpet sounds filled the air as the
elephant herd began to cheer.

Peanut smiled, glad to be home.
He was surrounded by the ones he loved
and he was excited to share with them
his journey and what he learned.

Vocabulary From the Story

accomplishment - something that has been achieved successfully

acknowledged - accept or admit that something is true

amplified - to make louder

bank - the edge of land along side a river or lake

beckoned - a gesture to encourage someone to come closer or to follow

clumsily - in a way that lacks skill

confidently - feeling or showing faith in oneself

demonstrated - to clearly show or explain

encouragement - to cheer or support someone

fascinated - to strongly attract

hesitantly - in an unsure manner or way

intrigued - desire to want to know more

perched - to sit on a branch

sequenced - a number of things that come one after another

skeptical - having doubts

Murphy Tyler is a mom, wanderer and E-RYT 200 yoga instructor. She is a writer and artist by nature. In her free time she is barefoot outside on nature walks or gardening. Murphy's goal is to encourage young readers to follow their dreams and create a life they truly love. Be on the look out for more books to come.

You can find Murphy on instagram: @murphy__tyler